THE
COCKROACH

First Love, Last Rites

In Between the Sheets

The Cement Garden

The Comfort of Strangers

The Child in Time

The Innocent

Black Dogs

The Daydreamer

Enduring Love

Amsterdam

Atonement

Saturday

On Chesil Beach

Solar

Sweet Tooth

The Children Act

Nutshell

Machines Like Me

THE
COCKROACH

Ian McEwan

JONATHAN CAPE

LONDON

1 3 5 7 9 10 8 6 4 2

Jonathan Cape, an imprint of Vintage,
20 Vauxhall Bridge Road,
London SW1V 2SA

Jonathan Cape is part of the Penguin Random House group of companies
whose addresses can be found at global.penguinrandomhouse.com.

Penguin
Random House
UK

First published in the United Kingdom by Jonathan Cape in 2019

penguin.co.uk/vintage

A CIP catalogue record for this book is available from the British Library

ISBN 9781529112924

Typeset in 12/17 pt Dante MT
by Integra Software Services Pvt. Ltd, Pondicherry

Printed and bound in Great Britain by Clays Ltd, Elcograf S.p.A.

Penguin Random House is committed to a sustainable future for
our business, our readers and our planet. This book is made from
Forest Stewardship Council® certified paper.

MIX
Paper from
responsible sources
FSC® C018179

To Timothy Garton Ash

This novella is a work of fiction. Names and characters are the product of the author's imagination and any resemblance to actual cockroaches, living or dead, is entirely coincidental.

ONE

That morning, Jim Sams, clever but by no means profound, woke from uneasy dreams to find himself transformed into a gigantic creature. For a good while he remained on his back (not his favourite posture) and regarded his distant feet, his paucity of limbs, with consternation. A mere four, of course, and quite unmoveable. His own little brown legs, for which he was already feeling some nostalgia, would have been waving merrily in the air, however hopelessly. He lay still, determined not to panic. An organ, a slab of slippery meat, lay squat and wet in his mouth – revolting, especially when it moved of its own accord to explore the vast cavern of his mouth and, he noted with muted alarm, slide across an immensity of teeth. He stared along the length of his body. His colouring, from shoulders to ankles, was a pale blue, with darker blue piping around his neck and wrists, and white buttons in a vertical line right down his unsegmented thorax. The light breeze that blew intermittently across it, bearing a not unattractive odour of decomposing food and grain alcohol, he accepted as his breath. His vision was unhelpfully narrowed – oh for a compound eye – and everything he saw was oppressively colourful. He was beginning to understand that by a grotesque reversal his vulnerable flesh now lay outside his skeleton, which was therefore wholly invisible to him. What a comfort it would have been to catch a glimpse of that homely nacreous brown.

All this was worrying enough, but as he came more fully awake he remembered that he was on an important, solitary mission, though for the moment he could not recall what it was. I'm going to be late, he thought, as he attempted to lift from the pillow a head that must have weighed as much as five kilos. This is so unfair, he told himself. I don't deserve this. His fragmentary dreams had been deep and wild, haunted by raucous, echoing voices in constant dissent. Only now, as this head slumped back, did he begin to see through to the far side of sleep and bring to mind a mosaic of memories, impressions and intentions that scattered as he tried to hold them down.

Yes, he had left the pleasantly decaying Palace of Westminster without even a farewell. That was how it had to be. Secrecy was all. He had known that without being told. But when exactly had he set out? Certainly it was after dark. Last night? The night before? He must have left by the underground car park. He would have passed the polished boots of the policeman at the entrance. Now he remembered. Keeping to the gutter, he had hurried along until he had reached the edge of the terrifying crossing in Parliament Square. In front of a line of idling vehicles impatient to pestle him into the tarmac, he made a dash for the gutter on the far side. After which, it seemed a week passed before he crossed another terrifying road to reach the correct side of Whitehall. Then what? He had sprinted, surely, for many yards and then stopped. Why? It was coming back to him now. Breathing heavily through every tube in his body, he had rested near a wholesome drain to snack on a discarded slice of pizza. He couldn't eat it all, but he did his best. By good luck it was a margherita. His second favourite. No olives. Not on that portion.

His unmanageable head, he discovered, could rotate through 180 degrees with little effort. He turned it now to one side. It was a small attic bedroom, unpleasantly lit by the morning sun, for the curtains had not been drawn. There was a telephone at his bedside, no, two telephones. His constricted gaze travelled across the carpet to settle on the skirting board and the narrow gap along its lower edge. I might have squeezed under there out of the morning light, he thought sadly. I could have been happy. Across the room there was a sofa and by it, on a low table, a cut-glass tumbler and an empty bottle of scotch. Laid out over an armchair was a suit and a laundered, folded shirt. On a larger table near the window were two box files, one sitting on top of the other, both coloured red.

He was getting the hang of moving his eyes, now that he understood the way they smoothly swivelled together without his help. Rather than letting his tongue hang out beyond his lips, where it dripped from time to time onto his chest, he found it was more comfortably housed within the oozing confines of his mouth. Horrible. But he was acquiring the knack of steering his new form. He was a quick learner. What troubled him was the need to set about his business. There were important decisions to be taken. Suddenly, a movement on the floor caught his attention. It was a little creature, in his own previous form, no doubt the displaced owner of the body he now inhabited. He watched with a degree of protective interest as the tiny thing struggled over the strands of pile carpet, towards the door. There it hesitated, its twin antennae waving uncertainly with all of a beginner's ineptitude. Finally, it gathered its courage and stumbled under the door to begin a difficult, perilous descent. It was a long way back to the palace, and there would be much danger along the way. But if it made it without being squashed underfoot, it would find, behind the palace panelling or below the floorboards, safety and solace among millions of its siblings. He wished it well. But now he must attend to his own concerns.

And yet Jim did not stir. Nothing made sense, all movement was pointless until he could piece together the journey, the events, that had led him to an unfamiliar bedroom. After that chance meal he had scuttled along, barely conscious of the bustle above him, minding his own business as he hugged the shadows of the gutter, though for how long and how far was beyond recall. What he knew for certain was that he reached at last an obstacle that towered over him, a small mountain of dung, still warm and faintly steaming. Any other time, he would have rejoiced. He regarded himself as something of a connoisseur. He knew how to live well. This particular consignment he could instantly place. Who could mistake that nutty aroma, with hints of petroleum, banana skin and saddle soap. The Horse Guards! But what a mistake, to have eaten between meals. The margherita had left him with no appetite for excrement, however fresh or distinguished, nor any inclination, given his gathering exhaustion, to clamber all the way over it. He crouched in the mountain's shadow, on the springy ground of its foothills, and considered his options. After a moment's reflection, it was clear what he must do. He set about scaling the vertical granite wall of the kerb in order to circumvent the heap and descend on its far side.

Reclining now in the attic bedroom, he decided that this was the point at which he had parted company with his own free will, or the illusion of it, and had come under the influence of a greater, guiding force. Mounting the pavement, as he did, he submitted to the collective spirit. He was a tiny element in a scheme of a magnitude that no single individual could comprehend.

He heaved himself onto the top of the kerb, noting that the droppings extended a third of the way across the pavement. Then, out of nowhere, there came down upon him a sudden storm, the thunder of ten thousand feet, and chants and bells, whistles and trumpets. Yet another rowdy demonstration. So late in the evening. Loutish people making trouble when they should have been at home. Nowadays, these protests were staged almost every week. Disrupting vital services, preventing ordinary decent types from going about their lawful business. He froze on the kerb, expecting to be squashed at any moment. The soles of shoes fifteen times his own length slammed the ground inches from where he cowered and made his antennae and the pavement tremble. How fortunate for him that at one point he chose to look up, entirely in the spirit of fatalism. He was prepared to die.

But that was when he saw an opportunity – a gap in the procession. The next wave of protesters was fifty yards away. He saw their banners streaming, their flags bearing down, yellow stars on a blue ground. Union Jacks too. He had never scuttled so fast in his life. Breathing hard through all the trachea on his body segments, he gained the other side by a heavy iron gate seconds before they were on him again with thunderclaps of hideous tramping, and now catcalls and savage drumbeats. Seized by mortal fear and indignation, an inconvenient mix, he darted off the pavement and, to save his life, squeezed under the gate into the sanctuary and relative tranquillity of a side street where he instantly recognised the heel of a standard issue policeman's boot. Reassuring, as ever.

Then what? He proceeded along the empty pavement, past a row of exclusive residences. Here he was surely fulfilling the plan. The collective pheromonal unconscious of his kind bestowed on him an instinctive understanding of his direction of travel. After half an hour of uneventful progress, he paused, as he was meant to do. On the far side of the street was a group of a hundred or so photographers and reporters. On his side, he was level with and close by a door, outside which stood yet another policeman. And just then, that door swung open and a woman in high heels stepped out, almost spearing him right through his ninth and tenth abdominal segments. The door remained open. Perhaps a visitor was arriving. In those few seconds Jim looked into a welcoming, softly lit hallway, with skirting boards somewhat scuffed – always a good sign. On a sudden impulse that he now knew was not his own, he ran in.

He was doing well, given his unusual circumstances, lying on this unfamiliar bed, to recall such details. It was good to know that his brain, his mind, was much as it had always been. He remained, after all, his essential self. It was the surprising presence of a cat that had caused him to run, not in the direction of the skirting boards, but towards the stairs. He climbed three and looked back. The cat, a brown and white tabby, had not seen him, but Jim considered it dangerous to descend. So began his long climb. On the first floor there were too many people walking along the landing, in and out of rooms. More prospect of being trodden to death. An hour later, when he reached the second floor, the carpets were being vigorously vacuumed. He knew of many souls who had been lost that way, sucked into dusty oblivion. No choice but to keep on climbing until— but now, suddenly, here in the attic, all his thoughts were obliterated by the harsh ringing of one of the bedside telephones. Even though he found that he could at last move one of his limbs, an arm, he did not stir. He couldn't trust his voice.

And even if he could, what would he say? I'm not who you think I am? After four rings the phone went silent.

He lay back and allowed his frantic heart to settle. He practised moving his legs. At last, they stirred. But barely an inch. He tried again with an arm, and raised it until it towered far above his head. So, back to the story. He had heaved himself up the last step to arrive breathless on the top landing. He squeezed under the nearest door into a small apartment. Usually, he would have made straight for the kitchen but instead he climbed a bedpost and, utterly depleted, crept under a pillow. He must have slept deeply for— but now, dammit, there came a tapping sound and before he could respond, the door to the bedroom was opening. A young woman in a beige trouser suit stood on the threshold and gave a brisk nod before entering.

'I tried phoning but I thought I'd better come up. Prime Minister, it's almost seven thirty.'

He could think of no response.

The woman, clearly an aide of some kind, came into the room and picked up the empty bottle. Her manner was rather too familiar.

'Quite an evening, I see.'

It would not have done to remain silent for long. From his bed he aimed for an inarticulate sound, somewhere between a groan and a croak. Not bad. Higher pitched than he would have wanted, with a hint of a chirrup, but plausible enough.

The aide was gesturing towards the larger table, at the red boxes. 'I don't suppose you had a chance to, uh . . .'

He played it safe by making the same sound again, this time on a lower note.

'Perhaps after breakfast you could take a . . . I should remind you. It's Wednesday. Cabinet at nine. Priorities for government and PMQs at noon.'

Prime Minister's Questions. How many of those he had crouched through, listening enthralled from behind the rotten wainscoting in the company of a few thousand select acquaintances? How familiar he was with the opposition leader's shouted questions, the brilliant non sequitur replies, the festive jeers and clever imitations of sheep. It would be a dream come true, to be *primo uomo* in the weekly operetta. But was he adequately prepared? No less than anyone else, surely. Not after a quick glance at the papers. Like many of his kind, he rather fancied himself at the despatch box. He would be fast on his feet, even though he only had two.

In the space where once he sported a fine mandible, the unwholesome slab of dense tissue stirred and his first human word rolled out.

'Righto.'

'I'll have your coffee ready downstairs.'

He had often sipped coffee in the dead of night on the tea room floor. It tended to keep him awake in the day, but he enjoyed the taste and preferred it milky, with four sugars. He assumed this was generally known by his staff.

As soon as the aide had left the room, he pushed away the covers and managed at last to swing his tuberous legs onto the carpet. He stood at last at a vertiginous height, swaying slightly, with his soft, pale hands pressed to his forehead, and groaning again. Minutes later, making his unsteady way towards the bathroom, those same hands began nimbly to remove his pyjamas. He stepped out of them to stand on pleasantly heated tiles. It rather amused him, passing water thunderously into a specially prepared ceramic bowl, and his spirits lifted. But when he turned to confront the mirror over the handbasin, they sank again. The bristling oval disk of a face, wobbling on a thick pink stalk of neck, repelled him. The pinprick eyes shocked him. The inflated rim of darker flesh that framed an array of off-white teeth disgusted him. But I'm here for a proud cause and I'll put up with anything, he reassured himself as he watched his hands turn the taps and reach for his shaving brush and soap.

Five minutes later he felt nauseated as he paused, still swaying, before the prospect of putting on the clothes laid out for him. His own sort took great pride in their beautiful, gleaming bodies and would never have thought to cover them up. White underpants, black socks, a blue and white striped shirt, dark suit, black shoes. He observed with detachment the automatic speed with which his hands tied his laces, and then, back at the bathroom mirror, his tie. As he combed his gingery brown hair, he noticed with sudden homesickness that it was the same colour as his good old shell. At least something has survived of my looks, was his melancholy thought as, finally, he stood at the top of the stairs.

He began a dizzying descent, trusting his legs to carry him down safely as he had his hands to shave and dress him. He kept a firm grip on the bannisters, smothering a groan at each step. As he crossed the landings, where there were hairpin turns, he clung on with both hands. He could have passed for a man with a hangover. But what had taken an hour to climb up took only seven minutes to climb down. Waiting for him in the hallway at the foot of the stairs was a group of very young men and women, each holding a folder. Respectfully they murmured, 'Good morning, Prime Minister,' in a soft, uneven chorus. None of them dared look at him directly while they waited for him to speak.

He cleared his throat and managed to say, 'Let's get on, shall we.' He was stuck for any further remark, but luckily a fellow, older than the rest and wearing a suit as expensive-looking as his own, pushed through and, seizing Jim by the elbow, propelled him along the corridor.

'A quick word.'

A door swung open and they went through. 'Your coffee's in here.'

They were in the Cabinet room. Halfway down the long table by the largest chair was a tray of coffee, which the prime minister approached with such avidity that over the last few steps he broke into a run. He hoped to arrive ahead of his companion and snatch a moment with the sugar bowl. But by the time he was lowering himself into the chair, with minimal decorum, his coffee was being poured. There was no sugar on the tray. Not even milk. But in the grey shadow cast by his saucer, visible only to him, was a dying bluebottle. Every few seconds its wings trembled. With some effort, Jim wrenched his gaze away while he listened. He was beginning to think he might sneeze.

'About the 1922 Committee. The usual bloody suspects.'

'Ah, yes.'

'Last night.'

'Of course.'

When the bluebottle's wings shook they made the softest rustle of acquiescence.

'I'm glad you weren't there.'

When a bluebottle has been dead for more than ten minutes it tastes impossibly bitter. Barely alive or just deceased, it has a cheese flavour. Stilton, mostly.

'Yes?'

'It's a mutiny. And all over the morning papers.'

There was nothing to be done. The prime minister had to sneeze. He had felt it building. Probably the lack of dust. He gripped the chair. For an explosive instant he thought he had passed out.

'Bless you. There was talk of a no-confidence vote.'

When he opened his unhelpfully lidded eyes, the fly had gone. Blown away. 'Fuck.'

'That's what I thought.'

'Where is it? I mean, where's the sense in—'

'The usual. You're a closet Clockwiser. Not with the Project. Not a true go-it-alone man. Getting nothing through parliament. Zero backbone. That sort of thing.'

Jim drew his cup and saucer towards him. No. He lifted the stainless steel pot. Not under there either.

'I'm as Reversalist as any of them.'

By his silence his special adviser, if that was what he was, appeared to disagree. Then he said, 'We need a plan. And quick.'

It was only now that the Welsh accent was evident. Wales? A small country far to the west, hilly, rain-sodden, treacherous. Jim was finding that he knew things, different things. He knew differently. His understanding, like his vision, was narrowed. He lacked the broad and instant union with the entirety of his kind, the boundless resource of the oceanic pheromonal. But he had finally remembered in full his designated mission.

'What do you suggest?'

There came a loud single rap, the door opened and a tall man with a generous jaw, bottle-black swept-back hair and pinstripe suit strode in.

'Jim, Simon. Mind if I join you? Bad news. Encryption just in from—'

Simon interrupted. 'Benedict, this is private. Kindly bugger off.'

Without a shift in expression, the foreign secretary turned and left the room, closing the door behind him with exaggerated care.

'What I resent,' Simon said, 'about these privately educated types is their sense of entitlement. Excluding you, of course.'

'Quite. What's the plan?'

'You've said it yourself. Take a step towards the hardliners, they scream for more. Give them what they want, they piss on you. Things go wrong with the Project, they blame anyone and everyone. Especially you.'

'So?'

'There's a wobble in the public mood. The focus groups are telling a new story. Our pollster phoned in the results last night. There's general weariness. Creeping fear of the unknown. Anxiety about what they voted for, what they've unleashed.'

'I heard about those results,' the prime minister lied. It was important to maintain face.

'Here's the point. We should isolate the hardliners. Confidence motion my arse! Prorogue parliament for a few months. Astound the bastards. Or even better, change tack. Swing—'

'Really?'

'I mean it. You've got to swing—'

'Clockwise?'

'Yes! Parliament will fall at your feet. You'll have a majority – just.'

'But the will of the p—'

'Fuck the lot of them. Gullible wankers. It's a parliamentary democracy and you're in charge. The house is stalled. The country's tearing itself apart. We had that ultra-Reversalist beheading a Clockwise MP in a supermarket. A Clockwise yob pouring milkshake over a high-profile Reversalist.'

'That was shocking,' the prime minister agreed. 'His blazer had only just been cleaned.'

'The whole thing's a mess. Jim, time to call it off.' Then he added softly, 'It's in your power.'

The PM stared into his adviser's face, taking it in for the first time. It was narrow and long, hollow at the temples, with little brown eyes and a tight rosebud mouth. He had a grey three-day beard and wore trainers and a black silk suit over a Superman T-shirt.

'What you're saying is very interesting,' the PM said at last.

'It's my job to keep you in office and this is the only way.'

'It'd be a ... a ...' Jim struggled for the word. He knew several variants in pheromone, but they were fading. Then he had it. 'A U-turn!'

'Not quite. I've been back through some of your speeches. Enough there to get you off the hook. Difficulties. Doubts. Delays. Sort of stuff the hardliners hate you for. Shirley can prepare the ground.'

'Very interesting indeed.' Jim stood up and stretched. 'I need to talk to Shirley myself before Cabinet. And I'll need a few minutes alone.'

He began to walk round the long table towards the door. He was coming to feel some pleasure in his stride and a new sense of control. Improbable as it had seemed, it was possible to feel stable on only two feet. It hardly bothered him to be so far off the ground. And he was glad now not to have eaten a bluebottle in another man's presence. It might not have gone down well.

Simon said, 'I'll wait for your thoughts, then.'

Jim reached the door and let the fingers of one strange hand rest lightly on the handle. Yes, he could drive this soft new machine. He turned, taking pleasure in doing it slowly, until he was facing the adviser, who had not moved from his chair.

'You can have them now. I want your resignation letter on my desk within the half hour and I want you out of the building by eleven.'

*

The press secretary, Shirley, a tiny, affable woman dressed entirely in black and wearing outsized black-rimmed glasses, bore an uncomfortable resemblance to a hostile stag beetle. But she and the PM got on well as she fanned out before him a slew of unfriendly headlines. 'Bin Dim Jim!' 'In the name of God, go!' Following Simon's usage and calling the hard-line Reversalists on the backbenches 'the usual bloody suspects' helped give the news a harmless and comic aspect. Together, Jim and Shirley chuckled. But the more serious papers agreed that a no-confidence vote might well succeed. The prime minister had alienated both the Clockwise and Reversalist tendencies within his party. He was too much the appeaser. By reaching out to both wings, he had alienated nearly everyone. 'In politics,' one well-known columnist wrote, 'bipartisan is a death rattle.' Even if the motion failed, ran the general view, the very fact of a vote undermined his authority.

'We'll see about that,' Jim said, and Shirley laughed loudly, as if he had just told a brilliant joke.

He was on his way out to sit by himself and prepare for the next meeting. He gave instructions to Shirley for Simon's resignation letter to be released to the media just before he stepped out into the street to deny to reporters that anything was amiss. Shirley expressed no surprise at her colleague's sacking. Instead, she nodded cheerfully as she gathered up the morning's papers.

It was bad form for all but the PM to be late for a Cabinet meeting. By the time he entered the room, everyone was in place round the table. He took his seat between the chancellor and the foreign secretary. Was he nervous? Not exactly. He was tensed and ready, like a sprinter on the blocks. His immediate concern was to appear plausible. Just as his fingers had known how to knot a tie, so the PM knew that his opening words were best preceded by silence and steady eye contact around the room.

It was in those few seconds, as he met the bland gaze of Trevor Gott, the chancellor of the Duchy of Lancaster, then the home secretary, attorney general, leader of the house, trade, transport, minister without portfolio, that in a startling moment of instant recognition, an unaccustomed, blossoming, transcendent joy swept through him, through his heart and down his spine. Outwardly he remained calm. But he saw it clearly. Nearly all of his Cabinet shared his convictions. Far more important than that, and he had not known this until now, they shared his origins. When he had made his way up Whitehall on that perilous night, he thought he was on a lonely mission. It had never occurred to him that the mighty burden of his task was shared, that others like him were heading towards separate ministries to inhabit other bodies and take up the fight. A couple of dozen, a little swarm of the nation's best, come to inhabit and embolden a faltering leadership.

There was, however, a minor problem, an irritant, an absence. The traitor at his side. He had seen it at a glance. In paradise there was always a devil. Just one. It was likely that among their number there was a brave messenger who had not made it from the palace, who had been sacrificed underfoot, just as he himself almost had, on the pavement outside the gates. When Jim had looked into the eyes of Benedict St John, the foreign secretary, he had come against the blank unyielding wall of a human retina and could go no further. Impenetrable. Nothing there. Merely human. A fake. A collaborator. An enemy of the people. Just the sort who might rebel and vote to bring down his own government. This would have to be dealt with. The opportunity would present itself. Not now.

But here were the rest, and he recognised them instantly through their transparent, superficial human form. A band of brothers and sisters. The metamorphosed radical Cabinet. As they sat round the table, they gave no indication of who they really were, and what they all knew. How eerily they resembled humans! Looking into and beyond the various shades of grey, green, blue and brown of their mammalian eyes, right through to the shimmering blattodean core of their being, he understood and loved his colleagues and their values. They were precisely his own. Bound by iron courage and the will to succeed. Inspired by an idea as pure and thrilling as blood and soil. Impelled towards a goal that lifted beyond mere reason to embrace a mystical sense of nation, of an understanding as simple and as simply good and true as religious faith.

What also bound this brave group was the certainty of deprivation and tears to come, though, to their regret, they would not be their own. But certainty, too, that after victory there would come to the general population the blessing of profound and ennobling self-respect. This room, in this moment, was no place for the weak. The country was about to be set free from a loathsome servitude. From the best, the shackles were already dropping. Soon, the Clockwise incubus would be pitchforked from the nation's back. There are always those who hesitate by an open cage door. Let them cower in elective captivity, slaves to a corrupt and discredited order, their only comfort their graphs and pie-charts, their arid rationality, their pitiful timidity. If only they knew, the momentous event had already slipped from their control, it had moved beyond analysis and debate and into history. It was already unfolding, here at this table. The collective fate was being forged in the heat of the Cabinet's quiet passion. Hard Reversalism was mainstream. Too late to go back!

TWO

The origins of Reversalism are obscure and much in dispute, among those who care. For most of its history, it was considered a thought experiment, an after-dinner game, a joke. It was the preserve of eccentrics, of lonely men who wrote compulsively to the newspapers in green ink. Of the sort who might trap you in a pub and bore you for an hour. But the idea, once embraced, presented itself to some as beautiful and simple. Let the money flow be reversed and the entire economic system, even the nation itself, will be purified, purged of absurdities, waste and injustice. At the end of a working week, an employee hands over money to the company for all the hours that she has toiled. But when she goes to the shops, she is generously compensated at retail rates for every item she carries away. She is forbidden by law to hoard cash. The money she deposits in her bank at the end of a hard day in the shopping mall attracts high negative interest rates. Before her savings are whittled away to nothing, she is therefore wise to go out and find, or train for, a more expensive job. The better, and therefore more costly, the job she finds for herself, the harder she must shop to pay for it. The economy is stimulated, there are more skilled workers, everyone gains. The landlord must tirelessly purchase manufactured goods to pay for his tenants. The government acquires nuclear power stations and expands its space programme in order to send out tax gifts to workers. Hotel managers bring in the best champagne, the softest sheets, rare orchids and the best trumpet player in the best orchestra in town, so that the hotel can afford its guests. The next day, after a successful gig at the dance floor, the trumpeter will have to shop intensely in order to pay for his next appearance. Full employment is the result.

Two significant seventeenth-century economists, Joseph Mun and Josiah Child, made passing references to the reverse circulation of money, but dismissed the idea without giving it much attention. At least, we know the theory was in circulation. There is nothing in Adam Smith's seminal *The Wealth of Nations*, nor in Malthus or Marx. In the late nineteenth century, the American economist Francis Amasa Walker expressed some interest in redirecting the flow of money, but he did so, apparently, in conversation rather than in his considerable writings.

At the crucial Bretton Woods conference in 1944, which framed the post-war economic order and founded the International Monetary Fund, there occurred in one of the sub-committees a fully minuted, impassioned plea for Reversalism by the Paraguayan representative Jesus X. Velasquez. He gained no supporters, but he is generally credited with being the first to use the term in public.

The idea was occasionally attractive in Western Europe to groups on the right or far right, because it appeared to limit the power and reach of the state. In Britain, for example, while the top rate of tax was still eighty-three per cent, the government would have had to hand out billions to the most dedicated shoppers. Keith Joseph was rumoured to have made an attempt to interest Margaret Thatcher in 'reverse-flow economics' but she had no time for it. And in a BBC interview in April 1980, Sir Keith insisted that the rumour was entirely false. Through the nineties, and into the noughties, Reversalism kept a modest profile among various private discussion groups and lesser-known right-of-centre think tanks.

When the Reversalist Party arrived spectacularly on the scene with its populist, anti-elitist message, there were many, even among its opponents, who were already familiar with the 'counter-flow' thesis. After the

Reversalists won the approval of the American president, Archie Tupper, and even more so when it began to lure voters away, the Conservative Party began, in reaction, a slow drift to the right and beyond. But to the Conservative mainstream, Reversalism remained, in the ex-chancellor George Osborne's words, 'the world's daftest idea'. No one knows which economist or journalist came up with the term 'Clockwisers' for those who preferred money to go round in the old and tested manner. Many claimed to have been first.

On the left, especially the 'old left', there was always a handful who were soft on Reversalism. One reason was that they believed it would empower the unemployed. With no jobs to pay for and plenty of time for shopping, the jobless could become seriously rich, if not in hoarded money, then in goods. Meanwhile, the established rich would be able to do nothing with their wealth other than spend it on gainful employment. When working-class Labour voters grasped how much they could earn by getting a son into Eton or a daughter into Cheltenham Ladies' College, they too began to raise their aspirations and defect to the cause.

In order to shore up its electoral support and placate the Reversalist wing of the party, the Conservatives promised in their 2015 election manifesto a referendum on reversing the money flow. The result was the unexpected one, largely due to an unacknowledged alliance between the working poor and the old of all classes. The former had no stake in the status quo and nothing to lose, and they looked forward to bringing home essential goods as well as luxuries, and to being cash rich, however briefly. The old, by way of cognitive dimming, were nostalgically drawn to what they understood to be a proposal to turn back the clock. Both groups, poor and old, were animated to varying degrees by nationalist zeal. In a brilliant coup, the Reversalist press managed to present their cause as a patriotic duty and a promise of national revival and purification: everything that was wrong with the country, including inequalities of wealth and opportunity, the north–south divide and stagnating wages, was caused by the direction of financial flow. If you loved your country and its people, you should upend the existing order. The old flow had merely served the interests of a contemptuous ruling elite. 'Turn the Money Around' became one of many irresistible slogans.

The prime minister who had called the referendum resigned immediately and was never heard of again. In his place there emerged a compromise candidate, the lukewarm Clockwiser James Sams. Fresh from his visit to Buckingham Palace, he promised on the steps of

Downing Street to honour the wish of the people. The money would be turned around. But, as many economists and other commentators had predicted in the low circulation press and unregarded, specialist journals, it was not so easy. The first and overwhelming question concerned overseas trade. The Germans would surely be happy to receive our goods along with our hefty payments. But they would surely not reciprocate by sending their cars to us stuffed with cash. Since we ran a trade deficit, we would soon be broke.

So how was a Reversalist economy to flourish in a Clockwise world? Negotiations with our most important trading partners, the Europeans, stalled. Three years went by. A mostly Clockwise parliament, torn between common sense and bending to the people's will, could offer no practical solutions. Sams had inherited a slim majority and flailed about between passionate factions in his party. Despite that, he was known to some newspapers as Lucky Jim, for it could have been far worse: Horace Crabbe, the leader of the opposition, was himself an elderly Reversalist of the post-Leninist left.

While Sams dithered, and his Cabinet remained divided along several lines of dissent, a purist faction on the Conservative backbenches was hardening its position. Britain must go it alone and convert the rest of the world by example. If the world failed to follow, so much the worse for it. This was ROC. Reversalism in One Country. Then the song and the graffiti were everywhere – Roc around the Clock. We had stood alone before, in 1940, after the fall of France, when German Nazi terror was engulfing Europe. Why bother with their automobiles now? But Sams held back, promising everything to all sides. Most economists, City journalists, business leaders and the entire financial sector predicted economic catastrophe if Sams went the way of the hard Reversalists. Banks, clearing houses, insurance brokers and international corporations were already relocating abroad. Eminent scientists, Nobel laureates, despaired in high-profile letters to the press. But on the street, the popular cry was lusty and heartfelt: get on with it! There was a mood of growing anger, a reasonable suspicion of having been betrayed. A newspaper cartoon depicted Jim Sams as Shakespeare's Gloucester, blinded, teetering on the chalk cliff's edge while Edgar, a tough John Bull Reversalist, urged him to jump.

Then, without warning and to general amazement, Sams and his wavering Cabinet seemed to find their courage. They were about to leap.

★

Once he had seen into all the pairs of eyes round the table, and as soon as he was confident of not bursting into joyful pheromonal song, the prime minister spoke some grave words of welcome. His voice was low and level. A muscle above his right cheekbone twitched repeatedly. No one had seen that before. During his introductory remarks he made a single passing reference to their shared identity when he spoke of this being a 'new' Cabinet which would from now on be voting as one in parliament. No more indiscipline. Blind collective obedience. There followed a sustained rustling and hum of assent around the table. They were of one mind, a colony of dedicated purpose.

Then business. On their way out, they would find copies of a recent survey of voter attitude which they should take away and read closely. They were to be mindful of one particular result: two thirds of those in the twenty-five to thirty-four age group longed for a strong leader who 'did not have to bother with parliament'.

'For now, we do,' Jim said. 'But ...' He let that hang and the room went still. He continued. 'The delayed Reversal Bill comes back to the house in three months. All opposition amendments will be voted down. Adaptation measures will start now. The chancellor will confirm, we'll be spending eight billion on transition arrangements.'

The chancellor, a frosty little fellow with pale grey eyebrows and a white goatee, smothered his moment of surprise and nodded sagely.

The prime minister returned the nod and gave a tight smile that did not part his lips. High reward. 'You should know now. I've fixed Reversalism day, R-Day, for the twenty-fifth of December, when the shops are closed. After that, the Christmas sales will be a colossal boost to GDP.'

He looked around. They were watching him intently. Not a single person doodling on one of the notepads provided. Jim raised his arms and locked his fingers behind his head, a peculiarly pleasant sensation.

'We'll be on course for quantitative easing, printing money so that the department stores can afford their customers and the customers can afford their jobs.'

The foreign secretary said abruptly, 'There's a developing situation in—'

The PM silenced him with a minimal shake of his head. He let his arms fall by his sides. 'Delivering R-Day, or Our Day as we might well call it, is our dedicated first priority. But our second is almost as important. Without it, the first could fail.'

He paused for effect. In that brief interval he had time to consider what to do with Benedict St John. His odd man out. A perfect murder was not easily arranged from Downing Street. One had been planned long ago from the House of Commons by that posturing top-hatted berk, Jeremy Thorpe. How that unravelled was warning enough.

'There'll be some bumps in the road ahead and we have to take the people with us. The focus groups are restive just when we need to be wildly popular. Vitally important. So, we'll be raising taxes for the low paid and lowering them for the rich. Big handouts for the workers after the twenty-fifth. To pay for that, as I'm sure our wise chancellor will agree, we'll increase government revenues by employing another twenty thousand policemen, fifty thousand nurses, fifteen thousand doctors and two hundred thousand dustmen to ensure daily collections. With their tax breaks, these new hires should easily be able to pay for their jobs. And the Chinese owe us eight hundred billion for the three nuclear power stations they'll be building.'

The attentive silence in the room appeared to shift, to downgrade in quality. No one trusted the Chinese government. Would they pay up? Would they put their own vast economy into reverse? Someone coughed politely. A few were examining their fingernails. If he had not quite lost the Cabinet's support, Jim realised he was in danger of earning its scepticism. He was saved by the minister for transport, an affable, pipe-smoking MP for a north-eastern constituency, believed to be fanatically ambitious.

'We'd save a lot of money by pressing ahead with the high-speed rail link to Birmingham.'

'Brilliant. Thank you, Jane.'

Emboldened, the muscular, square-jawed minister of defence Humphrey Batton said, 'And by commissioning four more aircraft carriers.'

'Excellent, Humph.'

'Ten thousand new prison places would bring in two and a half billion.'

'Well done, Frank.'

Suddenly, they were all at it, anxious to please, talking over each other by calling out departmental projects enabled by the new dispensation.

The PM sat back, beaming, letting the voices wash over him, occasionally murmuring, 'Jolly good … that's the spirit … tops!'

Inevitably, after a while, a feeling of exhaustion descended on the room, and into this lull the foreign secretary spoke.

'What about us?'

All heads turned respectfully towards Benedict St John. In that moment Jim realised that he was the only one who understood the man's unique status.

'What?'

The foreign secretary spread his palms to indicate an obvious point. 'Take my own case. But it could be yours. Next year I'm supposed to be in every capital in the world for Global Britain, persuading governments to come in with us. And I'm on a salary of £141,405 a year.'

'So?'

'With all my extended family responsibilities, it's simply too much to live on. How am I going to find time to do all the shopping to afford my job?'

Again, there was that quiet rustling sound beneath the table. Jim glanced around the room. Was Benedict being satirical? Perhaps he had spoken for all of them.

The prime minister stared at him in full contempt. 'Bloody hell, how should I ... you just, er ...'

It was the transport minister, Jane Fish, who once more helped him out.

'Go on Amazon, Bennie. One click. Get yourself a Tesla!'

A general sigh of relief at this elegant solution. The PM was ready to move on, but St John had not finished.

'I'm worried. On your R-Day the pound is likely to take a dive.'

Your? This was intolerable, but the PM managed a kindly look. 'That'll help our imports.'

'Exactly my point. Exports. We'll have to send even more money abroad.'

Jim explained as though to a child. 'Balanced by money we earn from imports.'

'In three years St Kitts and Nevis is all we have. Jim, this could be ruinous.'

Every minister was watching closely this direct challenge. The prime minister's sudden delighted laughter was genuine, for he had seen ahead, not only to the foreign secretary's inexplicable death, but to his funeral, a medium-grand affair at which Jim himself would deliver the peroration. St Paul's. Elgar's 'Nimrod'. The Horse Guards. Which reminded him, he had not yet had breakfast.

'Well, Benedict, as Karl Marx said, there's a lot of ruin in a nation.'

'It was Adam Smith.'

'All the truer for that.'

The ministers relaxed. They were disposed to take this last as a clincher, as a crushing remark. Jim drew breath to announce the next item.

But the foreign secretary said, 'Now to the important matter.'

'For God's sake, man,' the home secretary, Frank Corde, growled.

Benedict was sitting opposite the minister of defence. When the two men exchanged a glance, Batton shrugged and looked down at his hands. You tell them.

'It's a developing situation. No official statements as yet. But I'm told that the *Daily Mail* is about to run it on its website. So you all should know. I'm not usually—'

'Get on with it,' Jim said.

'Just after seven this morning a French frigate collided with the *Larkin*, one of our fishing boats off the Brittany coast, near Roscoff. Cut it in two. Crew of six. All pulled out of the drink.'

'Glad to hear it. So let's—'

'All drowned.'

The prime minister and his colleagues had grown up with death as a daily feature, with customary posthumous feasting as a hygienic necessity, as well as being a rather decent— he wrenched his thoughts away. He knew enough to allow a short silence before saying, 'Tragic. But things happen at sea. Why are we discussing this?'

'The boat was fishing illegally. In French coastal waters.'

'Well?'

The foreign secretary rested his chin on his hands. 'We were keeping this quiet while the relatives were being informed. But it broke on Twitter. The story going around now is the French rammed our boat deliberately. Enforcing their territorial rights.'

The chancellor of the Duchy of Lancaster said, 'What's the French line?'

'Thick fog, smallish wooden boat, two kilometres off-shore, transponder off for some reason. Didn't show on the frigate's radar. Our own naval data and other sources back up everything they're saying.'

'That's clear enough, then,' the attorney general said.

The foreign secretary looked at his watch. 'The *Mail* will be running a fighting piece this morning on their website. Patriotically outraged. Soon the story will be on all platforms. It's getting nasty. Fifty minutes ago, just as we were sitting down, someone put a brick through a window at the French embassy.'

He paused and looked at the prime minister. 'We need a statement from the highest level. Take the heat out of this nonsense.'

They all looked at Jim, who tipped back in his chair and said to the ceiling, 'Hmm.'

In a coaxing tone, Benedict added, 'Plus a call to the French president, with the conversation put on the record?'

'Hmm.'

They watched and waited.

At last he righted his chair and nodded at the Cabinet secretary, who customarily sat apart. 'If they're being buried together I want to be at the funeral.'

The foreign secretary started to say, 'That might seem a bit—'

'Hang on. Better than that. If the coffins are coming back together, and bloody well make sure they are, I intend to be there, quayside, airstrip, whatever.'

While the rest were frozen, not so much in outrage as fascination, the foreign secretary was trembling. He seemed to be about to stand, then sat again. 'Jim. You cannot do that.'

The prime minister appeared suddenly joyful. He adopted a breezy, mocking, see-saw voice. 'Now, Benedict, when this meeting breaks up, you're to go round the corner to your splendid office and do two things. You'll summon the French ambassador and demand an explanation. And you'll tell your press office what you're doing.'

The foreign secretary took a deep breath. 'We can't play games. This is a very close ally.'

'Six of our brave men have died. Until it's proved otherwise, I'm assuming this was a despicable assault.'

Finally, the secretary of state for defence found his courage. His voice had a throttled sound. 'Actually, the Admiralty data is pretty sound.'

'Admirals! Time servers, the lot of them. No doubt with farmhouses in the Dordogne to consider.'

This was good. Such an unfashionable English corner of France. There were chuckles round the table. The tight line of St John's jaw suggested he had nothing more to say. But the prime minister went on staring hard at him for almost thirty seconds. The effect on the rest was intimidating, in particular on Humphrey Batton, popular in the country for having once been a captain in the Second Paras. He found something of interest in his water glass on the table in front of him. He clasped it tightly between both hands.

'We'll get the Americans on side,' Jim said. 'They have special feelings for the French. Comments? Good. Now, moving on.' He took from his pocket a scrap of paper torn out from the *Spectator* magazine. On it was a pencilled list. 'To mark R-Day we'll mint a commemorative ten-pound coin. My idea is for a mirror image of a clock.'

'Brilliant ... wonderful idea,' was the collective response. The chancellor swallowed hard and nodded. Someone said, 'On the reverse, I assume.'

The prime minister glared about, looking for the culprit. The joke fell flat. 'Any other thoughts?'

There were none.

'Next. We'll institute an R-Day national holiday. The Christmas period's no good, obviously, so I'm going for the nearest date in the new year, January the second. Objections?'

'No,' they murmured.

'Good. That happens to be my birthday.'

At that, the entire Cabinet, except for the foreign secretary, applauded with slaps to the table.

Modestly, the prime minister held up a restraining hand and the room fell silent. In his short, previous existence he had never known such contentment. It seemed to him five years had passed, not three or four hours, since he had woken, sad and deranged, unable to control his limbs or even his tongue. He saw it in his colleagues' faces – he was in command, he was a force, here and in the land, and beyond. Hard to believe. Thrilling. Amazing. Nothing could stand in his way.

He glanced down at his list. 'Ah yes. I had this thought. The Reversalist movement needs a song, a positive one. An anthem of some sort. Something more with-it than "Ode to Joy". And it came to me. This old favourite from the sixties. "Walking Back to Happiness." You must know it. No? For God's sake, Helen Shapiro!'

They didn't know it, or her. But they did not dare shake their heads. Whatever secretly bound them, they were now immersed, lost to their respective roles. The cost of their ignorance was high, for the prime minister began to sing in a wavering baritone, with his arms spread wide and a forced grin like a practised crooner.

'Walking back to happiness, woopah oh yeah yeah.'

Nor did they dare catch each other's eye. They sensed that a misplaced smile could terminate a career. Nor, when the PM made a come hither wiggle with his fingers, did they dare not join the chorus. They sang in solemn unison 'Yay yay yay yay ba dum be do' as they might a hymn by Hubert Parry.

Even while in full throat, Jim saw that the foreign secretary was silent. Not even mouthing the words. He was staring straight ahead, immobile, perhaps with embarrassment. Or was it contempt?

When the singing came to a ragged end, St John stood and said to no one in particular, 'Well, I have things to do, as you know.' Without acknowledging the PM, he quickly left the room.

As he turned to watch him go, Jim was amazed at how it was possible to feel such joy and such hatred at the same time. A human heart, of which he was now in full possession, was a wondrous thing.

*

After he had brought the meeting to an end, Jim spent some minutes alone, working on his priorities statement. He gave some selected quotations to Shirley to shape into a press release. She worked quickly and well. By the time word came that his car was outside and the front door was opening for him, the press already had wind of something new and bold sweeping through his government. How fine it was to step out into daylight, to tower above the threshold he had crawled over the night before. Fine too, to hear the babble of excited questions shouted at him from the other side of the street. He paused by the front door, which had closed behind him, to give the photographers their half minute, but he did not speak. Instead, he raised a hand in friendly salute and gave the cameras a determined half smile. He was completely in command now of his binocular, non-mosaic, high-colour focused gaze, and he let it move slowly over the faces of the journalists, over the lenses, and then, as the Jaguar XJ Sentinel (an armoured car much to his taste) drew up and the door opened, he raised both hands in triumph, now grinning broadly, and stooped to slip onto the rear seat.

On the short ride down Whitehall to the Palace of Westminster, he had time to relish the moment ahead when he would stand at the despatch box to make the intentions of his government clear. What stirred him was the thought of the hidden, silent audience crouching behind the wainscoting. Even now they would be amassing in the darkness. How proud of him his family would be.

★

From *Hansard*, 19 September, Vol. 663 Priorities for Government

The Prime Minister (James Sams)

With permission, Mr Speaker, I shall make a statement on the mission of what is, in effect, a new Conservative government. When the bill returns to this house, Mr Speaker, our mission will be to deliver Reversalism for the purpose of uniting and re-energising our great country and not only making it great again, but making it the greatest place on earth. By 2050 it is more than possible, and less than impossible, that the UK will be the greatest and most prosperous economy in Europe. We will lie at the centre of a new network of reverse-flow trade deals. We will be the best on the planet in all fields. We will be the earth's home of the electric airplane. We will lead the world in not wrecking our precious planet. That same world will follow our shining example and every nation will reverse its money flow in order not to be left behind—*[Interruption.]*

Mr Speaker

Order. There is far too much noise in this Chamber. Too many members think it is all right for them to shout out their opinions at the prime minister. Let us be clear: it is not.

The Prime Minister

Mr Speaker, I applaud your intervention. This government is no longer divided. Myself and all the ministers are one body and we speak with one mind. We are formidable in our unity. The Bill will therefore pass. Nothing will stand in our way. We are turbocharging the civil service to prepare for the transition. We will move swiftly to accelerate and extend our trade deals beyond brave St Kitts and Nevis. Until that time, we proclaim

Reversalism in One Country. We will stand alone just as we have stood alone in the past. A lot of negativity about Reversalism has been wildly overdone. This is no time for faint Clockwise thinking. Let no one doubt it, the money flow is about to change direction – and about time, too. On day one, on R-Day, the beneficial effects will be felt on both macro and micro levels. On R-Day, for example, our newly empowered police might pull over a recklessly speeding motorist and hand through the window two fifty-pound notes. It will be that driver's responsibility, in the face of possible criminal charges, to use that money to work and pay for more overtime, or find a slightly better job. This is just one example, Mr Speaker, of how Reversalism will stimulate the economy, incentivise our brilliant citizens, and render our democracy more robust.

Reversalism will bless our future – clean, green, prosperous, united, confident and ambitious. When, together, we bend our sinews to the task, the dead hand of Clockwise economics and its vast bureaucracy of enterprise-denying rules and Health and Safety impediments will be lifted from us, all of us, one by one. And very soon, it will be lifted from all the nations on earth. We stand at the beginning of a golden age. Mr Speaker,

I commend this future to the house just as much as I commend this statement.

Several hon. Members rose—

Mr Speaker

Order.

[Continues.]

THREE

The youth who threw the brick at the French embassy that morning ran off and no arrest was made. This was noted in Paris. At the time of the incident, the crowd in Knightsbridge was estimated at around fifty. By late afternoon there were more than five hundred, some of whom were trawlermen who had travelled from Hull in buses laid on by the Reversalist Party. There were chants and shouts, but otherwise it was a peaceful demonstration. The five extra policemen drafted in had little to do but stand by the main doors of the embassy and watch. But just after four thirty someone threw 'an incendiary device'. It landed harmlessly on the damp grass by some laurels under a window and did not ignite. It was a milk bottle containing an inch or so of lighter fluid. It was reported as a petrol bomb, which may have been technically correct. This attack was also noted in Paris.

Earlier that afternoon, the French ambassador, Le Comte Henri de Clermont L'Hérault, was summoned to the Foreign and Commonwealth Office to account for the deaths of the six English trawlermen. The meeting was officially described as 'constructive', with the ambassador expressing sincere and heartfelt condolences to the families and profoundest apologies for the tragic accident. Little of this was picked up by the press, for the prime minister came out of Downing Street at 5 p.m. and made a statement of untypical resolve. The so-called bomb, deplorable as it was, had been examined and was a firework, in fact, 'a damp squib', and likely nothing more than a joke in extremely poor taste. Then Sams read out the names of the dead men, whom he described as 'English heroes'. He too expressed deepest condolences to the bereaved families and said that he was 'disturbed' by this tragic incident and was 'not wholly satisfied' with the explanations given by the ambassador earlier. The PM had heard expert advice. Modern technology, especially on an up-to-date naval vessel, was such that it was hard to understand how a thirty-foot fishing boat could not be detected in a fog, however thick. He understood that the skipper of the boat might not have known that he was inside French territorial waters and that he was fishing illegally. Sams accepted that in a rules-based international order, territorial rights must be respected. However – and here he paused – where violations occur, 'responses must be considered and appropriate'. He was therefore 'seeking further clarification from our very good friends, the French'. Refusing questions, he abruptly turned away and went back inside Number Ten.

In an instant, out of tragedy a diplomatic crisis was born. President Larousse, already baffled and irritated by *l'inversion britannique* and the disruption it threatened to French exports of wine and cheese to the UK, was, his spokesman said, 'disappointed' that the English should 'doubt the word of a very good friend'. That the Sams administration should imply that it was French government policy to 'murder innocent fishermen who wandered into our coastal waters was an insult to all that France holds dear'. Clearly, M. Sams, in difficulties over a decision that had divided his country, was positioning himself behind 'a nationalist wave of manufactured anger fed by an irrational Twitter storm'. Reluctantly, the president had decided to recall his ambassador. Le Comte Henri de Clermont L'Hérault would be returning to Paris for consultations.

Reasonably enough, Jim decided to recall the British ambassador in Paris. Things were shaping up well. In a difficult time such as this, the country needed a staunch enemy. Patriotic journalists praised the prime minister for facing down the French and speaking up for 'our lost boys'. The priorities statement to the Commons had also gone down well with important sections of the press. An opinion piece in the *Mail* was headlined, 'Who Put the Fire in Jim's Belly?'

At the end of that first, crowded day, the prime minister had retreated to his small apartment at the top of the building and busied himself with understanding Twitter, a primitive version, so he decided, of the pheromonal unconscious. He read Archie Tupper's recent output and began to suspect that the American president was, just possibly, 'one of us'. An obsequious fellow sent by a Whitehall IT team helped the PM open his own account. Within two hours he had 150,000 followers. An hour later, that number had doubled.

While he stretched out on the sofa, Jim found that a tweet was the perfect medium in which to reflect sagely on the Roscoff Affair, as it was now known. His first attempt was feebly derivative. 'Clockwiser Larousse is just a loser, and in my view the least effective French President in living memory.' *In my view* – as if there were others. Limp. And no calling it back. The following day the American president was awake early to head the debate from his bed and demonstrate how it was done. 'Tiny Sylvie Larousse sinking English ships. BAD!' It was poetry, smoothly combining density of meaning with fleet-footed liberation from detail. Larousse was emasculated, then diminished with a taunt that, true or not (his name was Sylvain, he was five foot nine), must forever be his badge; the fisherman's boat became a ship, the ship became ships; no tedious mention of the dead. The final judgement was childlike and pure, memorable and monosyllabically correct. And the parting flourish of those caps, that laconic exclamation mark! From the land of the free, here was a lesson in imaginative freedom.

Later, with pencil poised over notepad, Jim considered some refinements to the Reversalism Bill. He could see opportunities for criminals. Be unemployed, shop re-lentlessly, stuff a suitcase with cash, hop abroad to some dirty EU economy, open a bank account. Work to earn in Calais, shop to earn in Dover. Bastards. The solution was clear – it was happening anyway. The cashless soci-ety would create a digital trail for every pound earned in the shops, and every pound spent on work. Hoarding sums above twenty-five pounds would be a criminal of-fence, well advertised. Maximum sentence? Best not to be too harsh, not at first. So, five years.

He wrote notes at high speed in a neat copperplate, taking pleasure in forming the letters. An opposable thumb was not such a bad idea. Upstart young species like *Homo sapiens* sometimes came up with a useful development. As for the elaboration or broadcast of ideas, writing, despite its artisanal charm, was lugubriously analogue. He paused only once from his labours to devour a plate of parmigiana brought to him on a tray. He didn't bother with the salad.

Next. As soon as the bill was passed, his immediate concern must be to persuade the Americans to reverse their economy. From that, everything would follow. The Chinese would have to reverse in order to be able to afford their exports, so would Japan and the Europeans. Getting Tupper on board needed forethought, nice treats. Jim was on his fourth pages of notes. *Problem: AT not drinker/state visit softener/banquet with HM gold carriage flunkeys fanfares address parliament etc/Most Nob Order of Garter plus Vic Cross plus hon. knighthd/memship White's/gift Hyde Park as priv golf course.*

But the American president was a serious man of big tastes, with his own moral certitudes, by background not trained up to value the subtle ribbons-and-medals allure of the honours system. What were White's or Hyde Park to one who owned more expensive clubs and bigger courses? Who cared for 'Sir' when one was 'Mr President' for life? In the late afternoon of that day, the prime minister had given the matter some serious thought. He had set his staff to research certain legal niceties of the American system, and the extent of presidential power and how both might fare in a reverse-flow economy. Jim now had all he needed to know about article two of the US constitution. He was aware of the force of law and astonishing reach of a presidential executive order. Like most people, he already knew that the president was also the commander-in-chief of the United States Armed Forces. The Cabinet Office had provided Jim with a general overview of the process by which the American defence budget was negotiated and effected. He had in his notes the precise figure in billions of dollars for the year ahead. The attorney general had come to Downing Street to explain the position. The US president could, by his own order, devolve the defence budget as agreed by congress, to his own office. By standard Reversalist processes, funds would flow back up the system, from the army, navy and air force personnel, and all their suppliers and all the manufacturers, directly to the president. Seven hundred and sixteen billion dollars would be his.

'Personally his? Legally his?' Jim had asked the attorney general.

'Legally, yes. It would set a precedent that might surprise his opponents. But with this president, most people have grown accustomed to surprises.'

'Let me be clear,' Jim said. 'He could bank that money?'

'Of course. Cayman Islands, perhaps. The Russian president should be able to help. Even at low interest rates he could live reasonably well on seven or eight billion a year without touching the capital.'

'What about US defences?'

The attorney general laughed. 'Congress would ratify the budget again. These days, they love borrowing money.'

But now, as Big Ben up the road sounded a dolorous eleven o' clock, Jim worried how he would pitch this on the phone. Tupper was not one for the simple life. Would 716 billion do it? Should he suggest the president appropriate the education budget? Along with healthcare? But that might require three executive orders. Too complicated. He would have to take a chance. It was 6 p.m. in Washington. The president would be busy watching television and might not appreciate the interruption. Jim hesitated a few more seconds, staring into the swirl of encrusted colour, purplish reds and creamy whites, on his empty dinner plate, then phoned down to tell the night staff to put through an unminuted call.

It took them twenty-five minutes to exchange identification protocols, enable the voice scrambling encryption, and get the president's attention, and another ten to patch him through. Not bad for an unscheduled conference.

'Jim.'

'Mr President. I hope I'm not disturbing you in the middle of important—'

'No, just, um ... I hear you're sticking it to the French.'

'They murdered six of our lads.'

'Murder isn't good, Jim.'

'Absolutely. I couldn't agree more.'

For an anxious moment their accord drained the exchange of purpose. Jim could hear down the line shouts and pistol shots in the background and the neighing of many horses, then a sudden change of scene, expansive orchestral music with French horns and strings, suggestive of open desert with cacti and buttes. He cast around for safe small talk. 'How is Mel—'

But the president spoke over him. 'What's the latest with, you know, that thing, the Revengelism project?'

'Reversalism? Fantastic. We're almost ready to go. Great excitement over here. It's a historical turning point.'

'Shake things up is good. Give the EU a bad time.'

'Mr President, this is what I wanted to discuss with you.'

'You got two minutes.'

So the prime minister laid out the matter in the terms his attorney general had used, adding some colourful plumbing and weather imagery of his own. Up the pipes came a counterflow surge of newly released energy that explosively blew old thinking, blasted old blockages aside and at the end, the release point or outlet, there shot up high into the air a fabulous fountain of trade deals and also funds, electronic dollars that fell earthwards like longed-for rain, like a storm of spiralling autumn leaves, like a vortex-blizzard of snowflakes pouring down into . . .

'My account?' the president said in a husky voice. 'You're saying into my business account?'

'Offshore, of course. You should get your own people to check.'

A silence, broken only by the rippling sound of TV laughter, and of a honky-tonk piano and the clinking of glasses, and celebratory gunfire.

Finally, 'When you put it that way I can see there might be something in it. Definitely. I think together we could make Revengelism work, Jim. But now I've got to, um . . .'

'One last thing, Mr President. May I ask you something personal?'

'Sure. As long as it's not about—'

'No, no. Of course. It's about ... *before*.'

'Before what, Jim?'

'Six?'

'Say again.'

'All right. Are you ... Did you once ... '

'Once what?'

'Have, erm ...'

'Jesus! Get it out, Jim! Have what?'

It came in a whisper. 'Six legs?'

The line went dead.

*

The weather, that dependable emblem of private and national mood, was in turmoil. A five-day, record-breaking heatwave was followed by two weeks of record-breaking rain across the entire country. Like all the lesser rivers, the Thames rose, and Parliament Square languished under four inches of water and much floating plastic and waxed-cardboard detritus. The best photographers could not make the scene picturesque. As soon as the rains stopped, a tall heat strode in from the Azores once more and a second, longer heatwave began. For a week, as the floodwaters receded, there was thick smooth silt under foot everywhere in riverine London. The humidity never fell below ninety per cent. When the mud dried, there was dust. When the scorching winds blew, which they did with unusual ferocity and for days on end, there were novel urban sandstorms, brownish yellow, thick enough to obscure from view Nelson on his column. Some of the sand, it turned out on analysis, came from the Sahara. A live black scorpion four inches long was found in a consignment of fresh dates on sale in Borough Market. It was impossible to persuade feverish social media that these venomous creatures were not wind-born, and had not breezed in from north Africa on a south-westerly. A deluge of scorpions had biblical echoes. Real or not, they added to the profound unease among the substantial minority of the electorate convinced that a catastrophe was at hand, driven by a government of reckless ideologues. Another substantial minority, slightly larger, believed that a great adventure was at hand. It could hardly wait for it to start. Both factions were represented in parliament, though not in government. The weather was right. Turmoil and reduced visibility was everywhere.

Unhelpfully, the French released the dead fishermen in their coffins one by one, after post mortems, over a week. They were flown to Stansted, not the sort of airport Jim wished to be seen in. The dead, at government insistence, were not released immediately to the families. Instead, they were held in cold storage outside Cambridge and when the last man had been brought in from France, all six were flown to Royal Wootton Bassett by an RAF transport plane. Jim took charge of the planning. He decided that there would be no brass band. Instead, he would stand alone on the airstrip, silently facing a camera crew and the massive four-engine propeller plane as it taxied to a stop. A brave lonely figure confronting the giant machine. Jim's antennae were finely attuned to public sentiment. As it happened, it was the first day of the heavy rains. The coffins, draped in Union Jacks, were brought out in single file, by members of the Grenadier Guards, marching in funereal slow step, and placed at the prime minister's feet. The rain played well. He correctly refused an umbrella as he stood to attention in the downpour. Were those tears on his face? It was reasonable to think so. The nation came together in a passing frenzy of grief. In Hull and near HMS *Belfast* in London, flowers, teddy bears and toy fishing boats were piled forty feet high.

Then came the second heatwave. Tucked under a baking roof, its windows shut tight against the gritty winds, the prime minister's apartment warmed to an extraordinary level. But Jim was energised by the moist heat. He had never felt healthier. His blood, excited and thinned, raced through and nourished his busy mind with fresh ideas. He had refused to replace Simon with a new special adviser. He had also dispensed with Cabinet meetings. Delivering Reversal was his only purpose, to which his every sinew was bent, just as he had promised in parliament. Reversalism consumed him and he no longer knew why or how. He entered a state of barely conscious bliss, unaware of time or hunger or even his own identity. He was deliriously obsessed, burning with strange passion, hot with impatient desire for explanations, details, revisions. Prompted by a dim recollection of Churchill in 1940, he appended to every written directive, 'Report back to me today to confirm the above has been accomplished.' These words were made available to the press. The prime minister took meetings with the heads of MI5 and 6, business and trade union leaders, doctors, nurses, farmers, headmasters, prison governors and university vice chancellors. Preferring not to take questions, he patiently explained how their different sectors would blossom in the new regime. He had regular consultations with the chief whip. It looked like the Reversalism Bill would pass easily with a margin of twenty votes or so. The PM wrote memos, issued commands, and made motivating phone calls to his ministerial team. He sent down inspirational press statements to Shirley. The civil service was now properly turbocharged; across London the lights were on all night in the ministries. And in the Downing Street apartment too. Outside, by day and night, dispatch riders lined up to collect or deliver documents too confidential to be entrusted to digital transfer.

Developments further afield were also good. A British-owned farmhouse in Provence was daubed with red paint by French patriots. The London tabloids were healthily inflamed. When the prime minister held President Larousse personally accountable, the figure of a club-wielding John Bull with Jim's face appeared in a *Sun* cartoon and was widely circulated on the Internet. In the polls, Sams was up fifteen points over Horace Crabbe. In his early morning tweets, the American president described Prime Minister Sams as 'a great man' and announced that it was time to reverse the entire US economy. Before lunch, a thousand points were wiped off the Dow Jones. The next morning, Tupper changed his mind. He was, he said, just 'playing with the idea'. Stock markets around the world were reassured. When the chairman of the Federal Reserve dismissed Reversalism as 'loopy', the President doubled back in anger. Reversalism was on again. It would bring 'the old elite to its knees'. This time the Dow Jones was untroubled. As one Wall Street insider said, the markets would panic when it was time to panic.

It was Gloria, the young woman in the trouser suit who had come to wake Jim on that first morning, who tapped on the door late one evening to deliver the news. Simon had been found hanged by a tow-rope in the bedroom of his house in Ilford, where he lived alone. Even better, there was no note. He had been dead for at least a week. While Gloria went down to find some champagne, Jim wrote a quick note of praise and regret. It was good of Simon not to be writing a memoir or plotting with enemies of the Project. Gloria said her goodnight and took the warm encomium – deeply moving, everyone would say – downstairs for Shirley to type up and send out. The prime minister drank the bottle alone while he continued with his work. But his usual concentration was just a little diminished. Something was nagging at him, a little un-coiling thread of suspicion that he couldn't quite justify. At last, he had to put down his pen to think this through. It came down to nothing more than trivial superstition that he, the most rational of creatures, could not dismiss: there had been nothing but good news lately – the exhilarating pace of work, the chief whip's calculations, the collapse of the 1922 Committee revolt, the dead fishermen, his press, his soaring popularity, the red paint, Tupper's praise and now this. Was he being so unreasonable when the experience of a lifetime demonstrated that any torrent of delightful fortune must at some point be checked? At the end of his rope, Simon had made the prime minister nervous. He slept poorly, worrying all night that this happy death presaged a turning point.

And so it did, the next morning, not one point but two, each turning in the same direction. The first came in the form of an early morning email from the chief whip. There was a secret cabal among his own backbenchers, a group of Clockwisers who had been meeting in a private house somewhere outside London. Not much was known about them, their numbers or their names. There were obvious candidates, but no evidence, only bland denials. They had voted with the government so far to conceal their identities. It was a mystery or a miracle, the way they had dodged the attentions of the whips' office. But one thing was now known for sure. The foreign secretary, Benedict St John, was the moving force and it was suspected that the intention was to help the opposition defeat the Reversalism Bill when it came back to the Commons.

This ugly disloyalty was on the PM's mind as he shaved and dressed and descended the stairs. In his fury, he wanted to hit someone, or break something. It was an effort to appear pleasant when his junior staff greeted him in the hallway. He had been too preoccupied, too complacent. He should have dealt with Benedict St John days ago. If only he was a free agent, Jim would happily have taken an axe to the man's throat. These furious, violent thoughts did not begin to fade until he sat down to his coffee and his tight-lipped press secretary laid before him the *Daily Telegraph*'s double-page spread.

It was one of those leaks from within the heart of government in which the paper excelled, hardly seeming to care how this one went against the grain of its strict Reversalist line. The allure of a scoop was total. This was a well-laid-out reduction of a Royal Navy memo that revealed the Roscoff Affair to have been an accident. It was hard to doubt it: radar and satellite data, ship-to-shore intercepts, rescue divers to frigate intercepts, French embassy and Élysée Palace intercepts, and eye-witness reports. Jim read it over twice. Nothing here that Simon could ever have had access to. Among the many diagrams and photographs was a picture of himself, rain-sodden and erect on the airfield tarmac by the flag-covered coffins. The leak was a political calculation, and clearly a Clockwise-inspired attack. The source was obvious. These two bad developments were related. His enemies were on the move and Reversalism was under threat. Jim knew he had to act quickly.

Shirley's office had already prepared a press statement. Jim read it through, deleting all hints of apology to the French. It was a decent holding position. He was giving no interviews. Essentially, the prime minister was immensely relieved to hear that what happened to the crew of the *Larkin* was the consequence of a tragic accident. Here, from our courageous Royal Navy, was the irrefutable proof that the French government, for reasons of their own, had been unable to provide. The terrible loss suffered by the families of the lost crew remained a matter of deep, etc... bereaved, etc. The prime minister thanked the French authorities for all their etc., etc., and wished to reassure our good neighbour that routine intercepts of their radio and telephone traffic was no more than a sincere expression of the UK's profound esteem. Etc., etc., etc., for the Fifth Republic.

He signed off on the text and, on his way back upstairs, told his staff that he was not to be disturbed. In the apartment he locked the door, cleared papers from the coffee table and placed at its centre a large notepad and a red ink biro. He sat, hesitating, chin in hand, then began to write names, draw circles round them, link the circles with single or double lines embellished with arrows and question marks. He appraised actions and their possible consequences, their discoverability and their deniablity through the distorting prism of alliances, rupture and disgrace. His was a perfectly pitched and balanced mind, well adapted by inheritance over unimaginable stretches of time to the art of survival and the advancement of his kind. Also, a life of constant, almost routine struggle had perfected in him effortless mastery in defending all that he possessed – while seeming not to. He was calm in the knowledge that he would prevail. And in this moment of scheming, he was richly self-aware, fully alive to the joy of politics at its purest, which was the pursuit of ends at all costs. He thought and calculated hard, and after half an hour it was clear to him that it was too late to commission the foreign secretary's murder. He turned to a fresh blank page, and considered.

There were other, gentler forms of murder. Contemporary social life was a metaphorical armoury of newly purposed weapons, of tripwires, poisoned darts, land mines waiting for a careless step. This time Jim did not hesitate. It took him two hours to write his article, possibly for the *Guardian*, a confession of sorts that demanded of its author the trick, entirely alien to him, of inhabiting another's mind. He persevered and within three paragraphs was already beginning to feel sorry for himself, or for the self he would have to find and cajole. Or threaten. It was an open-ended scheme. Only by writing it could it be discovered. When he was done, he walked up and down within the confined attic space in a state of exultation. There was nothing more liberating than a closely knit sequence of lies. So this was why people became writers. Then he sat again with his hand hovering near the phone. There were three names on his list. Whom could he trust? Or, whom did he mistrust the least? Even as he set himself the question he knew the answer, and his forefinger was already tapping the keys.

*

The one thing everybody knew about Jane Fish was that she smoked a pipe. Everybody also knew that, actually, she didn't. She wasn't even a smoker. Years ago, starting out in the humblest, most wretched, least popular job in government, secretary of state for Northern Ireland, she had attended an event in Belfast for an anti-smoking charity. She agreed to take one puff on a pipe and blow the smoke into the face of a child to highlight the dangers of secondary smoking. The little girl's eyes were closed and she did not inhale. But public life is lived in broad strokes. The customary two-day media storm followed. Since Fish was outspoken and often in the news and had a pleasant, unexceptional face, cartoonists had no choice but to keep the pipe in her mouth. For political sketch writers, she would be forever 'pipe-smoking Jane Fish'. She was popular. In the spectrum of available opinion, she belonged mostly in the no-nonsense faction and was well liked for her stand against breastfeeding in public. She had been a passionate Clockwiser until, respectful of the will of the people, she became a passionate Reversal-ist. She was admired for speaking well for both.

Of the three women on his list, she was, in the prime minister's view, the closest to her pheromonal roots. His judgement was good. On the phone that night, when he laid out the facts, she understood immediately the need for firm action. She confided that she'd always had her doubts about Benedict. Jim had his hand-written article biked round to her immediately in a sealed pouch. She phoned back ninety minutes later with her suggested changes. Some concerned matters of historical detail, others were what she called 'a matter of voice'. The fol-lowing morning, Shirley typed up the messy manuscript and went round to King's Cross to deliver it to and nego-tiate with the editor of the *Guardian*. The prime minister had insisted that the press secretary was to remain on the premises while the piece went into production. This was a broad-minded paper that had once run a column on its opinion pages by Osama bin Laden, and employed as a journalist a paid-up member of Hizb ut-Tahrir, an extremist organisation. It was a bit of a stretch to run a piece by Jane Fish, but how could a Clockwise paper resist when one minister was destroying another in a government it despised?

It is a wonderful sight, deeply stirring, when a great newspaper has only a few hours to get behind an important story. Immense expertise and teamwork, long memories and rapid analysis come nobly into play. The whole building hums. Shirley told her staff later that it was like being in a frontline hospital at the height of a bloody battle. The entire front page was turned around, along with three pages inside, and a leader by the editor herself. By five that afternoon, the first copies were coming off the presses. That may have been a high moment for older journalists, to hold a fresh hard copy in their hands. But it was irrelevant. By then, the paper's website had been running the revelations, with constant updates, for four hours. Plenty of time for rival papers to pick up the story for tomorrow's editions, and for evening television news to rejig their running orders. Social media, blogs, political webzines were on fire. The Roscoff Affair, with its niggling historical details of murders that turned out to have been mere accidents, drifted down the lists. If the prime minister had pointed the finger at the French, he was only as mistaken as everyone else. No skulduggery off the Brittany coast, but plenty here in Whitehall. A holder of one of the great offices of state was in disgrace. Where was the foreign secretary? When was he going to resign? How would the government handle the crisis? What did this mean for Reversalism? When were powerful men going to reform their ways? To this last, the prime minister had a single-word answer.

FOUR

It was 2,857 words long, and written more in regret than vengefulness. This was a tale of harassment, bullying, obscene taunts and inappropriate touching that led by turns to verbal abuse. That Fish went out of her way to stress that no actual rape took place gave her account added veracity. That the blunt, plain-speaking northerner should relate these matters with such raw sensitivity moved some to tears. Even a subeditor was wet-eyed. The appalling events related to a twenty-month period fifteen years before, when Jane Fish was parliamentary private secretary to Benedict St John and he was minister for work and pensions. She had suffered ever since, too fearful for her career, too humiliated to speak out and strangely protective of her gifted colleague. She was breaking silence now because the foreign secretary's youngest child was eighteen and because she had come to believe she had a duty to younger women who occupied vulnerable positions like the one she once had. The front page headline was, 'Foreign Secretary's Shame'. A contemporary photograph showed Fish following St John onto a train, carrying his luggage. Around the body of the piece were boxed texts of explanation and analysis. In her leader, the editor deplored such vile behaviour, but cautioned against a rush to judgement. On the opinion page a younger member of the *Guardian* staff decreed that the victim was not only always right, but had a right to be believed.

Reading his copy of the paper that afternoon, alone in the Cabinet room, the prime minister found himself, on balance, siding with the latter. The more he read over his own work and admired the layout, the more convincing it became. He had to hand it to Jane. Such vicious, ruthless, heartless lying. Such an insult to real victims of masculine power. He wondered if he himself would ever have dared put his name to the article. Framed and confined within these pages, the story generated its own truth, rather in the way he imagined a nuclear reactor produced its own heat. Whether these things had happened or not, they might well have, they could so easily have, they were bound to have. They had! He was beginning to feel indignant on Jane's behalf. The foreign secretary was a wretch. Worse than that, he was late.

Five minutes later, when St John was shown in, Jim was still reading the pages, ostentatiously now, pen in hand. The two men did not exchange a greeting, nor did the prime minister stand. Instead he indicated the chair opposite him. At last, he folded the paper away, sighed and shook his head sadly. 'Well ... Benedict.'

The foreign secretary made no reply. He continued to stare steadily at Jim. It was disconcerting. To fill the silence the PM added, 'I'm not saying I believe a word of this.'

'But?' St John prompted. 'You're about to say but.'

'I am indeed. But, but and but. This isn't good for us. You know that. Until it's cleared up, I need you out the way.'

'Of course.'

There was silence again. Jim said kindly, 'I know how it used to be. Bit of malarkey behind the filing cabinet. Different times now. Me Too and all. There's your but. You have to go. That's final. I need your letter.'

St John reached across the table, pulled the newspaper towards him and opened it out. 'You were behind this.'

The PM shrugged. 'You leaked to the *Telegraph*.'

'Ours was all true. But yours!'

'Ours is true now, Benedict.' Jim glanced at his watch. 'Look, am I going to have to sack you?'

The foreign secretary took out a piece of paper folded in four and tossed it on the table.

Jim spread it out. Standard stuff. Great honour to have served ... baseless allegations ... distraction from the invaluable work of government.

'Good. So. Spend more time with your plotters.'

Benedict St John didn't even blink. 'We're going to fuck you up, Jim.'

In such exchanges it was important to have, if not the last word, then the last little touch. As the prime minister stood, he pressed a button under the table. It had been carefully arranged. A heavily bearded policeman came in, carrying an automatic rifle.

'Take him out the front way. And go slowly,' Jim said. 'Don't release his elbow until he's through the gates.'

The two men shook hands. 'They're waiting for you out there, Bennie. A photo-op. Would you like to borrow a comb?'

*

There was nothing in the near-infinite compendium of EU rules and trade protocols of the customs union that prevented a member state from reversing the circulation of its finances. That did not quite represent permission. Or did it? It was a defining principle of an open society that everything was lawful until there was a law against it. Beyond Europe's eastern borders, in Russia, China and all the totalitarian states of the world, everything was illegal unless the state sanctioned it. In the corridors of the EU, no one had ever thought of excluding the reverse flow of money from acceptable practice because no one had ever heard of the idea. Even if someone had, it would have been difficult to define the legal or philosophical principles by which it should be illegal. An appeal to basics would not have helped. Everyone knew that in every single law of physics, except one, there was no logical reason why the phenomena described could not run backwards as well as forwards. The famous exception was the second law of thermodynamics. In that beautiful construct, time was bound to run in one direction only. Then Reversalism was a special case of the second law and therefore in breach of it! Or was it? This question was hotly debated in the Strasbourg Parliament right up until the morning the members had to decamp to Brussels, as they frequently had to. By the time they had arrived and unpacked and enjoyed a decent lunch, everyone had lost the thread, even when a theoretical physicist came specially from the CERN laboratories to set everything straight in less than three hours with some interesting equations. Besides, the next day a further question arose. Would what the scientist said remain true if he'd said it in reverse?

The matter, like many others, was set aside. A fierce debate on Moldovan ice cream was pending. The issue was not as trivial as the Europhobe London press was pretending. The struggle to harmonise the ingredients of the high-quality Moldovan product with EU rules represented a microcosm of growing diplomatic tensions between the west and Russia over the future of the tiny, strategically placed country. It was a complex business but, in theory at least, it was solvable. Reversalism was beyond all that.

The average Brussels official had watched in wonder as the startling decision was made by referendum. Then, after all, one tended to relax and shrug as the whole process predictably stalled, mired in complexity. Surely, this nonsense was about to be shelved in the time-honoured fashion. But lately there was even greater wonder as kindly, dithering Prime Minister Sams appeared to undergo a personality change to emerge as a modern Pericles, artful and ferocious in driving Reversalism through, do or die, with or without Europe. Was it really going to happen? Couldn't the mother of parliaments bring the nation to its senses? Could it really be the case that a fellow from Brussels in need of recreation could spend a lavish weekend at the London Ritz, then walk away from the check-out desk with three thousand pounds in his hand? And perhaps be arrested the same day for being in possession of illegal funds? Or at the least, have his funds confiscated as he left the country? Or – what horror – be obliged to buy a job in the hotel kitchens washing dishes until the cash was spent? How could a nation do this to itself? It was tragic. It was laughable. Surely the Greeks had a word for it, choosing to act in one's own very worst interests? Yes, they did. It was *akrasia*. Perfect. The word began to circulate.

But the puzzled, weary or condescending smiles began to freeze when the tweets of the US president assumed a degree of consistency on the subject. In the name of free trade, American prosperity and greatness, and raising the poor, Reversalism was 'good'. Prime Minister Sams was great. And, although by the conventions of EU subsidiarity this was strictly an internal affair, it bothered some in Brussels that President Tupper was proposing an ex-general, the billionaire owner of a string of casinos, to be the new 'czar' of the British National Health Service. For these various reasons the prime minister was listened to with unusual courtesy when he delivered a lecture at NATO headquarters in early December.

Sams was there in place of his disgraced foreign secretary. There was nothing new of substance in his talk except for its urgency. The PM came straight to the point. As everybody knew, the UK would be reversing its finances and therefore its fortunes on the twenty-fifth of that month. 'Save the date!' he called out cheerily. There were obliging smiles. The prime minister ran through a list of demands, long familiar to the negotiators among the audience in the grand lecture hall. The first of the EU's new annual contributions to the UK of £11.5 billion would fall due on 1 January. Nato's first payment was not expected until June. The funds that would accompany all EU exports to the UK must assume an inflation rate of two per cent. And to repeat – and here Jim spread his hands as though to embrace them all – as a gesture of goodwill, funds accompanying UK exports to the EU would match that rate. There were further technicalities as well as reassurances about the United States' 'direction of travel'. In his closing remarks, Jim expressed the hope that before long 'the scales would drop from your eyes', a phrase that flummoxed the Bulgarian interpreter in her booth at the back of the hall. The scales would drop, the prime minister said, and everyone would 'follow us blindly into the future'.

Afterwards, a young French diplomat was overheard saying to a colleague as they made their way to the banquet, 'I don't understand why they stood to applaud. And so loudly, and for so long.'

'Because,' his older companion explained, 'they detested everything he said.'

It was not unreasonable for the British press to describe Jim's speech as a triumph.

There was a disconcerting moment the next day in Berlin. He was there for a private meeting with the chancellor. It was a busy day for her in the Reichstag and, with much apology, she met with him in a tiny sitting room near her office. Apart from two interpreters, two notetakers, three bodyguards, the German foreign minister, the British ambassador and the second secretary, they were alone. Where they sat, an ancient oak table separated the two leaders. Everyone else was obliged to stand. Over the chancellor's shoulder the PM had a view across the Spree towards a museum. Through its plate glass windows, he could see a display of the history of the Berlin Wall. Jim knew two words in German: Auf and Wiedersehen. Halfway through the meeting, he was setting out his stall. He wanted extra funds to accompany German exports of cars to the UK in return for extra funds to supplement British exports of Glaswegian

Riesling which, as he explained, was far superior to the Rhenish version.

It was at this point that the chancellor interrupted him. With her elbow on the table, she pressed a hand to her forehead and closed her tired eyes. '*Warum?*' she said, and followed this word with a brief tangle of others. And again, '*Warum ...*' and a longer tangle. Then the same again. And finally, still with her eyes closed, and her head sinking a little further towards the table, a simple, plaintive, '*Warum?*'

Tonelessly, the interpreter said, 'Why are you doing this? Why, to what end, are you tearing your nation apart? Why are you inflicting these demands on your best friends and pretending we're your enemies? Why?'

Jim's mind went blank. Yes, he was weary from so much travel. There was silence in the room. Across the river a line of schoolchildren was forming up behind a teacher to go into the museum. Standing right behind his chair, the British ambassador softly cleared her throat. It was stuffy. Someone should open a window. There drifted through the PM's mind a number of compelling answers, though he did not utter them. Because. Because that's what we're doing. Because that's what we believe in. Because that's what we said we'd do. Because that's what people said they wanted. Because I've come to the rescue. Because. That, ultimately, was the only answer: *because*.

Then reason began to seep back and with relief he recalled a word from his speech the evening before. 'Renewal,' he told her. 'And the electric plane.' After an anxious pause, it came in a rush. Thank God. 'Because, Madame Chancellor, we intend to become clean, green, prosperous, united, confident and ambitious!'

That afternoon he was on his way back to Tegel Airport, dozing in the back of the ambassador's limo, when his phone rang.

'Bad news, I'm afraid,' the chief whip said. 'I've threatened all I can. They know they'll be deselected. But a dozen or more have gone over to Benedict. Sacking has made him popular. And they don't believe Fish. Or they hate her anyway. The way things stand now we're more than twenty votes short ... Jim, are you there?'

'I'm here,' he said at last.

'So.'

'I'm thinking.'

'Prorogue *pour mieux sauter*?'

'I'm thinking.'

He was gazing out of the bulletproof window. The driver, preceded and followed by the outriders, was taking a circuitous route down narrow green roads, past well-kept shacks with quarter-acre gardens, also nicely tended. Little second homes, he assumed. There was a particular greyness to Berlin. A smooth and pleasant grey. It was in the air, in the light sandy soil, in the speckled stonework. Even in the trees and grass and suburban herbaceous borders. It was the cool and spacious grey necessary to sustained thought. As he mused and the chief whip waited, Jim felt his heartbeat slowing and his thoughts arranging themselves into patterns as neat and self-contained as the little houses he was passing. It was as if he was in possession of an ancient brain that could solve any modern problem it confronted. Even without the deep resource of the pheromonal unconscious. Or of the trivial Internet. Without pen and paper. Without advisers.

He looked up. The procession of cars and motorbikes ushering the prime minister towards his waiting RAF jet had stopped to rejoin the main road. Just then, a question came to him. It seemed to drift up from the bottom of a well a hundred miles deep. How lightly and beautifully it rose to present itself. How easy it was to pose the question: who was it he loved most in all the world? Instantly, he knew the answer, and he knew exactly what he was going to do.

★

No one was surprised when Archie Tupper asked a business friend to organise an impromptu conference of Re-
publican lawmakers and the various institutes and think
tanks to which they were attached. These meetings were
common, rather devout, well funded, patriotic and con-
vivial. The general drift was pro-life, pro-second amend-
ment, with a strong emphasis on free trade. Mining,
construction, oil, defence, tobacco and pharmaceuticals
were well represented. Jim now recalled that he himself
had been a couple of times, before he became leader of
the party. He had only fond memories of affable, portly
types of a certain age, with their scented, closely shaven
pink faces, gentlemen comfortable in their tuxes. (Few
women attended and no people of colour.) One kindly fellow had pressed on him a generous invitation to a
million-acre ranch in Idaho. Five minutes later, another
promised him a welcome in an antebellum spread in
Louisiana. Generous and friendly, they tended to be
hostile to any mention of climate change and to international organisations like the UN, NATO and the EU.
Jim had felt at home. It was inevitable that they would
take a close interest in and help fund Britain's Reversalist
project, though many thought it was better suited to a
small country and not for the USA. But perhaps Tupper
was about to convince them otherwise. British MPs of

the right persuasion had often been invited in the past couple of years. But this hastily arranged conference was going to make reverse-flow finance its theme. The president would give a brief keynote speech. Among the international guests invited were forty pro-government Conservative MPs. The venue was a hotel in Washington that happened to belong to Archie Tupper, which was expected to give proceedings there a certain intimacy.

For the British contingent, the timing was inconvenient. The parliamentary timetable was full. The only conversation was Reversalism. There was much anxiety about the rebellion led by the treacherous ex-foreign secretary. The date set for the vote was 19 December. Constituency business always intensified around this time, and there were the usual Christmas engagements, as well as family gatherings. But this was a luxurious trip, first-class travel, suites measuring six thousand square feet, astonishing five-figure per diem expenses, a handshake with the president and overall excitement that American interest in the British Project was growing. On top of that, the prime minister had written to them all personally, urging them to attend. He wasn't going himself. Instead he was sending in his place Trevor Gott, the chancellor of the Duchy of Lancaster, a dull fellow, occasionally impulsive, often described as being 'two-dimensional'. There was nothing for it – the MPs made their apologies to colleagues, constituency officials and families and set about making their 'pairing' arrangements. This was a parliamentary convention by which a member who had to be absent from the house for a vote could pair off with an MP of the opposing benches. Neither would attend, and so the vote could not be affected. It was particularly useful for MPs on the government side who were often away on official business. Useful too for MPs who were ill or demented or attending funerals.

The conference was a stunning success, as they almost always are. At the start, President Tupper said that the British prime minister was great, and Reversalism was good. Among the congressmen and senators, oligarchs and think-tank intellectuals, there was a joyous sense that the world was configuring itself to their dreams. History was on their side. The banquet on the evening of 18 December was as magnificent as the several banquets that preceded it. After the speeches, a full orchestra backed a Frank Sinatra imitator in a soaring rendition of 'My Way'. Then a Gloria Gaynor lookalike brought seven hundred tearful diners to their feet with 'I Will Survive'.

Just as everybody was sitting down, the phones of forty guests vibrated in unison. They were urgently commanded by the chief whip to return to London. Their ground transport was already outside the hotel. Their flight was leaving in two hours. They had ten minutes to pack. They were needed in the Commons by eleven the next morning for the crucial Reversalism vote. The pairing arrangement had broken down.

The British left the banqueting room with no time for farewells to their new friends. How they cursed their Labour colleagues all the way to Ronald Reagan Airport. What an outrage, to be dragged from paradise by the perfidy of those they had foolishly trusted. Since most of the MPs were too angry to sleep, they punished the drinks trolley and cursed all the way to Heathrow. Due to heavy traffic around Chiswick, they arrived in the Commons just a few minutes before the Division Bell rang. Only as the Washington Revellers, as they came to be known, filed through the lobby did they notice the absence of their pairing partners. The Bill was passed with a majority of twenty-seven votes. The rest, as people kept saying all through the morning, was 'history'. The next day, the Reversalism Bill received Royal Assent and passed into law.

It was, of course, a constitutional scandal, a disgrace. Howls of rage from the Clockwiser press. The forty paired Labour MPs signed a letter to the *Observer* angrily denouncing the Sams government's 'filthy, shameless manoeuvrings'. There were calls for a judicial review.

'We'll ride it out. It will be fine. Just you see,' Jim told Jane Fish on the phone. Afterwards, he arranged for a case of champagne to be sent round to the chief whip's office.

That evening he gave a long interview to BBC television. He said in grave, reasonable tones, 'Apologise? Let me explain the fundamentals. In this country we do not have a written constitution. What we have instead are traditions and conventions. And I have always honoured them, even when to do so has been against my best interests. Now, I should point out to you that there is a long and honourable tradition in the house of breaking the pairing arrangement. Not so long ago, but before my time as prime minister, a Liberal Democrat MP was giving birth to her baby while her pairing partner, on the instruction of the whips, was voting in the Commons on a closely contested matter. As is well known, back in 1976 the highly respected Michael Heseltine picked up and swung the mace in the Chamber in celebration, one might say, of a broken pair. Twenty years later three of our MPs were paired not only with three absent Labour MPs but also with three Lib Dems. Labour has broken the pairing arrangement on countless occasions. They're only too happy to tell you about it late at night in the Strangers' Bar. All these examples bind into place a convention of cheating that has passed into common practice. It is constitutionally correct. It shows the world that parliament is, above all, a fine and fallible place, warm and vibrant with the human touch. I should also add that pairing is far less common in important votes. It was quite right to bring those MPs back from Washington to the Commons when a matter of vital national importance was at stake. Of course, the opposition is crying foul. That's their job. Some of them are miffed that Horace Crabbe voted with us. So, in answer to your question, no, emphatically no, neither I nor any members of my government have anything to apologise for.'

It wasn't a white Christmas, but it was not far off. There was a light fall on the first of January, just before the R-Day bank holiday. Two inches of snow deterred no one. Millions rushed to the stores to lay in money to pay for their jobs when they returned to work after the break. There were a few expected teething problems. Fans turned up for a Justin Bieber concert expecting to be paid. The event was cancelled. People stood by cash machines wondering whether they were supposed to poke cash into the slot formerly intended for debit cards.

But these were the largest January sales on record. Shops were stripped clean of goods – a great boost to the economy some thought. The news that St Kitts and Nevis was withdrawing from the trade deal was barely noticed.

The prime minister, still in the Christmas spirit and looking rakish in a pink paper crown, sprawling shoeless in an armchair, neat whisky in hand, watched, along with a few of his staff, helicopter shots of mile-long queues along Oxford Street. He would have liked to say it out loud, but he let the words murmur in his thoughts: it was over; his job was done. Soon he would assemble his colleagues and inform them that it was time to begin the long march to the palace and be welcomed as heroes by their tribe.

*

In the afternoon, before the last Cabinet meeting, the PM sent all the staff home and arranged for the policeman on the front door to keep it ajar. All Cabinet members were to leave their borrowed bodies tidily at their ministry desks, ready for the return of their rightful owners. Jim left his own body on the bed upstairs. Thus, for the meeting itself, he imposed a strict dress code: exoskeletons. He had thought it would be fitting to convene on the Cabinet room table, but once they had assembled in the room, it looked an awfully long way up and rather tricky, since the table legs were highly polished. So they gathered in a corner of the room behind a wastepaper bin and stood in a proud circle. The PM was about to launch on his opening remarks but was cut off by a rendition of 'Happy Birthday', sung in lusty unharmonious chirrups. Afterwards they looked nervously towards the door. The duty policeman had not heard them.

The Cabinet meeting was conducted in pheromone, which runs at ten times the speed of standard English. Before Jim could speak, Jane Fish proposed a vote of thanks. She praised the PM's 'single-mindedness coupled, unusually, with rambunctious charm and humour.' Britain now stood alone. The people had spoken. The genius of our party leader had got them over the line. Their destiny was in their hands. Reversalism was delivered! No more dithering and delay! Britain stood alone!

As she called out the beloved slogans she was overcome with emotion and could not go on, but it did not matter. Rising applause, an earnest susurration of carapaces and vestigial wings greeted her words. Then each Cabinet minister added a few words, ending with the new foreign secretary, Humphrey Batton, recently promoted from the Ministry of Defence. He led every-body in a round of 'For He's a Jolly Good Fellow'.

To give his speech, the PM stepped into the centre of the circle. As he spoke, his antennae quivered with passion and he rotated slowly on the spot to catch every-one's attention.

'My dear colleagues, thank you for these kind thoughts. They touch me deeply. In these closing mo-ments of our mission, our duty is to the truth. There is one that we have never concealed from our brilliant citizens. For the mighty engines of our industry, finance and trade to go into reverse, they must first slow and stop. There will be hardship. It might be punishing in the extreme. I don't doubt that enduring it will harden the people of this great country. But that is no longer our concern. Now that we have cast off our temporary, uncongenial forms, there are deeper truths that we may permit ourselves to celebrate.

'Our kind is at least three hundred million years old. Merely forty years ago, in this city, we were a margin-alised group, despised, objects of scorn or derision. At best, we were ignored. At worst, loathed. But we kept to our principles, and very slowly at first, but with gather-ing momentum, our ideas have taken hold. Our core be-lief remained steadfast: we always acted in our own best interests. As our Latin name, *blattodea*, suggests, we are creatures that shun the light. We understand and love the dark. In recent times, these past two hundred thousand years, we have lived alongside humans and have learned their particular taste for that darkness, to which they are not as fully committed as we are. But whenever it is predominant in them, so we have flourished. Where they have embraced poverty, filth, squalor, we have grown in strength. And by tortuous means, and much experiment and failure, we have come to know the preconditions for such human ruin. War and global warming certainly and, in peacetime, immoveable hierarchies, concentrations of wealth, deep superstition, rumour, division, distrust of science, of intellect, of strangers and of social cooperation. You know the list. In the past we have lived through great adversity, including the construction of sewers, the repulsive taste for clean water, the elaboration of the germ theory of disease, peaceful accord between nations. We have indeed been diminished by these and many other depredations. But we have fought back. And now, I hope and believe that we have set in train the conditions of a renaissance. When that peculiar madness, Reversalism, makes the general human population poorer, which it must, we are bound to thrive. If decent, good-hearted, ordinary people have been duped and must suffer, they will be much consoled to know that other decent, good-hearted, ordinary types like ourselves will enjoy greater happiness even as our numbers grow. The net sum of universal wellbeing will not be reduced. Justice remains a constant.

'You have worked hard on our mission these past months. I congratulate and thank you. As you have discovered, it is not easy to be *Homo sapiens sapiens*. Their desires are so often in contention with their intelligence. Unlike us who are whole. You have each put a human shoulder to the wheel of populism. You have seen the fruits of your labour, for that wheel is beginning to turn. Now, my friends, it is time to make our journey south. To our beloved home! Single file please. Remember to turn left as you go out the door.'

He did not mention it, but he knew that every minister in his Cabinet understood the perils that lay ahead. It was just after 4 p.m. on a cloudy afternoon when they slipped through the open door and past the duty policeman. They welcomed the winter gloom. Because of it, they did not see the little creature scurrying towards Number Ten to resume its life. Within half an hour Jim's group was passing under the gates of Downing Street into Whitehall. They crossed the pavement and climbed down into the gutter. The mountain of horse dung had long gone. The moving forest of rush-hour feet thundered above them. It took ninety minutes to reach Parliament Square and it was here that tragedy struck. They were waiting for the lights to change and were preparing to make their dash across the road. But Trevor Gott, the chancellor of the Duchy of Lancaster, got ahead of himself, as he sometimes did, and ran out too soon and disappeared under the wheel of a rubbish truck. When the traffic stopped the entire Cabinet ran out into the road to help him. He lay on his back, truly two-dimensional. From under his shell, there was extruded a thick, off-white creamy substance, a much-loved delicacy. There would be a heroes' banquet that night and what fun it would be, with so many extraordinary stories to tell. Before the lights changed again, his colleagues had just enough time to pick him up and place the extrusion reverently on his underbelly. Then, with six ministers each taking a leg, they bore him away to the Palace of Westminster.